Lizard in a blizzard

Lesley Sims

Illustrated by David Semple

Lizard is reading his book in the sun.

He looks up and grins at his friends.

This book's fun!

"It's all about snow, but what's snow? Do you know?"

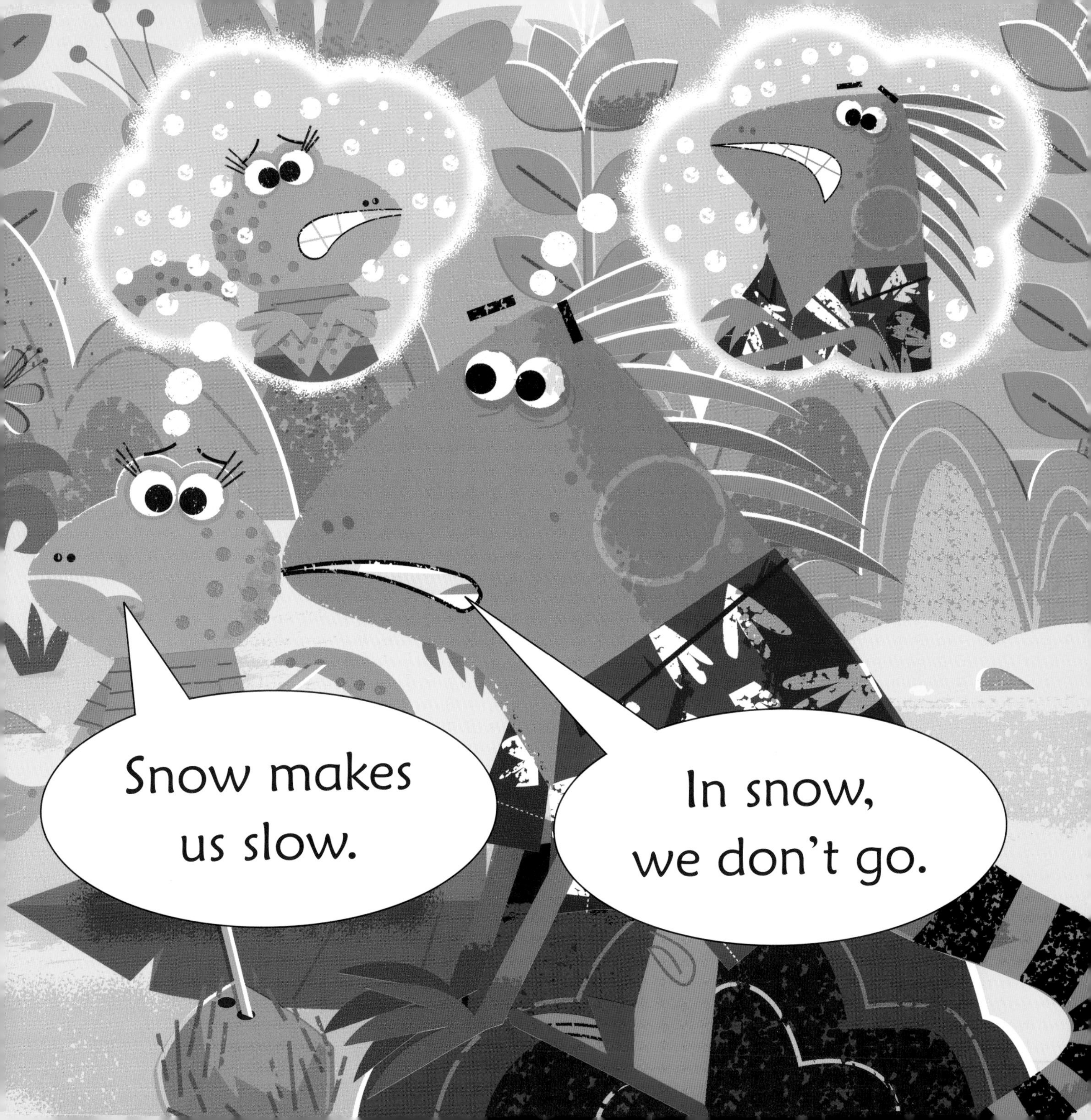
Snow makes us slow.
In snow, we don't go.

"I want to see snow," Lizard says, with a sigh.

"I want to make snowflakes float down from the sky."

He isn't a wizard but Lizard is clever.

He loves to put all sorts
of odd stuff together.

The next day, he shows them his
'Make snow!' invention.

He flicks up a switch
and his friends pay attention.

Softly at first, fat white flakes flutter down.

"How pretty!" says Gecko...

...but she soon starts to frown.

Lizard is shivering. "I don't know how!"

The flakes whirl down faster.
The world is a blur.

Reach out for each other!

The machine freezes up.

All at once, the storm ends.

Hot sun warms them all,
melting snow from the friends.

For six sunny days,
Lizard mends his
machine...

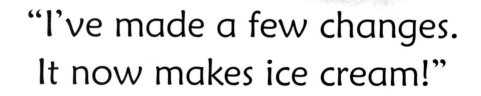

"I've made a few changes.
It now makes ice cream!"

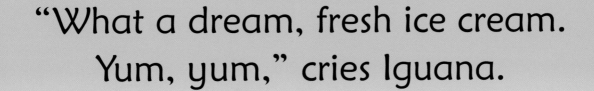

"What a dream, fresh ice cream.
Yum, yum," cries Iguana.

"Your ice cream is scrumptious –
chocolate chip and banana!"

"Thank you, Gecko," says Lizard.

He takes it and shakes it.
"Hurray – a warm blizzard!"

About phonics

Phonics is a method of teaching reading which is used extensively in today's schools. At its heart is an emphasis on identifying the *sounds* of letters, or combinations of letters, that are then put together to make words. These sounds are known as phonemes.

Starting to read
Learning to read is an important milestone for any child. The process can begin well before children start to learn letters and put them together to read words. The sooner children can discover books and enjoy stories and language, the better they will be prepared for reading themselves, first with the help of an adult and then independently.

You can find out more about phonics on the Usborne Very First Reading website, **www.usborne.com/veryfirstreading** (US readers go to **www.veryfirstreading.com**). Click on the **Parents** tab at the top of the page, then scroll down and click on **About synthetic phonics**.

Phonemic awareness

An important early stage in pre-reading and early reading is developing phonemic awareness: that is, listening out for the sounds within words. Rhymes, rhyming stories and alliteration are excellent ways of encouraging phonemic awareness.

In this story, your child will soon identify the *z* sound, as in **his** and **freezing**. Look out, too, for rhymes such as **ends – friends** and **iguana – banana**.

Hearing your child read

If your child is reading a story to you, don't rush to correct mistakes, but be ready to prompt or guide if he or she is struggling. Above all, do give plenty of praise and encouragement.

Edited by Jenny Tyler
Designed by Sam Whibley

Reading consultants: Alison Kelly and Anne Washtell

First published in 2018 by Usborne Publishing Ltd., Usborne House, 83-85 Saffron Hill, London EC1N 8RT, England.
www.usborne.com Copyright © 2018 Usborne Publishing Ltd.